Genny in a Bottle

how to create the boy of your dreams

how to create the boy
of your dreams

Kristen Kemp

an apple paperback

SCHOLASTIC INC.

New York Toronto London Auckland Sydney
Mexico City New Delhi Hong Kong

ISBN 0-439-21181-6

Copyright © 2001 by Kristen Kemp.
All rights reserved. Published by Scholastic Inc.
SCHOLASTIC and associated logos are trademarks and/or registered trademarks of Scholastic Inc.

12 11 10 9 8 7 6 5 4 3 2   1 2 3 4 5 6/0

Printed in the U.S.A.
First Scholastic printing, April 2001

To David Levithan, an excellent editor and wonderful friend. There would be no Genny without you.

Chapter 1

"The Best Addition to My Collection"

by Andrew

The day was sane when it started.

I got up, showered with Irish Spring, brushed my teeth, and gargled with mouthwash. As usual, the Listerine stung my mouth so badly that I wound up spattering some onto the mirror. I don't know why I keep using that stuff — I make a big mess with it every morning. It's just that I am a firm believer in fresh breath. If you have a minty mouth, that's when something interesting will happen. Like you'll wind up ear to ear with a teacher who's telling you some good, juicy gossip about what's going to be on her next test. Or even better, a cool, funky kid will start up a conversation and ask you to a great party. Or sometimes my classmates whisper that they want me to write their papers for them, and they offer me big-time money. Or, if the planets are all aligned just right — and if I keep dreaming and wishing hard enough — this rock star of a girl named MacKenzie will actually talk to me. (And what if she wants to kiss me on some faraway date? Well, she'll find out that I have the best breath in all of Sarasota plus the surrounding counties.) Oooooh, MacKenzie and me. She is a god; and I am not. I mean, I'm probably okay and all — but I just don't possess divine status like she does.

But back to fresh breath . . . I am particularly glad that I had it today. You never know when you're going to meet an amazing-looking genie.

Before school, I had some time on my hands, so I took the long way to Manatee Junior High on my banana-seat bicycle. I went straight to the oceanfront row of mansions. I stopped in the alleyways, where plum-filled trash cans of the rich and famous gleamed at me. Why would I do this? I love to — um, okay, I'll admit it to you — find treasures in other people's trash cans. I have come across some way-cool finds. For example, there were three Babe Ruth baseball cards buried inside an old shoe box. They were in perfect condition, and I sold them online for, oh my, a whole, whole lot. The best days are usually when I find fashion and sewing stuff for my good friend Gus. He loves to make the latest looks for everyone at school. (I'm not kidding — I'll explain later.) For Jane, my other good friend, I am always on the hunt for people's old fishing nets. Jane loves to catch the most colorful critters in the ocean, take their pictures, then throw them back. I keep trying to give her this great aquarium I found, but she won't take it. She doesn't think it's right for fish to be kept in a tank.

I totally agree with you if you think my friends are unique. I guess that's why I fit in with them so well.

So I found all kinds of crazy loot this morning. But that's not unusual; I have an eye for killer trash. For example, I brought home so many discarded computer parts that I put together my very own computer — and it works. I am trying to put one of my garbage-can computers together for Jane, too. (Gus already has a good one.) I often find designer purses that my mother loves and old military junk that my dad collects. But the craziest thing I found was this supernatural bottle. I've never found anything with special powers before.

I reached deep into a garbage can because I saw something bright and shiny beaming out of the forest-green Rubbermaid container. I shut my eyes, pinched my nose, and used my free hand to pull the piece of glass out. It turned out to be an ancient-looking urn or bottle. I rubbed it a few times to clean it off. (Someone's peanut butter sandwich had done a number on the interesting little thing.) Just as I was trying to figure out whether to keep the old bottle, I had quite a surprise.

I bet you can guess what it was.

Chapter 2
"Let Me out of the Loony Bin!!!"
by Genny the Genie

"You no-good excuse for a genie! Didn't you know that ponytails are, like, last decade? I mean, ya need a perm or an updo like mine," the voice screeched from inside the teeny-tiny bottle that was inside my bottle. "What's the matter? You scared of a little bleach? Let me outta here and I'll show you how to use some bleach."

"Eat *MY EARWAX*, Rebecca," I said, fishing for my state-of-the-art earplugs that still didn't help. My poor, formerly fat cat — who was now skinny because recently Rebecca had so cruelly tried to starve him — was begging me to buy him some kitty-plugs. See, this chick named Rebecca from Texas, the ex-genie we recently trapped and captured (to save the world from terror and wickedness), was turning our peaceful lives into a horror movie. She hadn't stopped screaming once in the four weeks since we first caught her. I don't know how she did it — her voice never even got scratchy. At least her put-downs were getting rusty. Because she'd been spouting off insults and obscenities (her mother — and mine — would be appalled!) for a month straight, her personal affronts were getting lamer by the second. That didn't mean they were any less annoying.

"Genny, someone should have named you Ninny. You're the worst excuse for a genie I have ever met in my life," she screamed at high volume.

"Okay, I heard you the first three hundred times!"

I was trying to tell Catfish about all of the genie-mails from our old friends, but it was impossible. My kitty and I had to yell as loud as fire engines whenever we wanted to say anything to each other. That crazy ex-genie was making our existence inside Throttle (my bottle) impossible. I knew exactly what she was trying to do, though; she didn't get anything past me. She thinks if she can scream nonstop, she'll drive us so crazy that we'll set her free. Rebecca's not smart or slick; it's like someone bleached her brain. But she has no idea how tolerant Catfish, Throttle, and I can be.

After more than 1,000 years together, we have gotten way good at putting up with difficult things.

"Genny, I think you stink. It would be nice if you took a bath every once in a while," she screamed some more. "It's cruel and unusual to live in pure crustiness."

"SHUT UP, REBECCA, SHUT UP!" I banged on her bottle. Catfish was afraid I was shaking it too hard, so he bit me. He's worried that one of these days I'm going to crack the glass, and she'll be out of the bag (or bottle, I should say). Believe me, the last thing the world needs is a free Rebecca.

Rebecca was right about one thing — I hate to admit it — it did stink inside Throttle. "Have you been eating too much garlic lately?" I asked my bottle. "Geez. It's starting to really smell ripe in here." In typical Throttle fashion, he ignored me. This time he had a good excuse, though. There was no way he could hear me over all the screaming.

Catfish was prancing around with Q-Tips sticking out of each ear. He swore it muffled the sound. He says Q-Tips can do magic things. Well, that never works for me.

At that very moment, *nothing* was working for me. I was not so sure I wanted to save the world anymore. I mean, I did a good thing and rid the earth of a very powerful, very evil new genie. And I got this for it?

I couldn't take it.

"Genny, I need some clippers so I can cut my toenails. Then I want to rub my toe fuzz IN YOUR FACE!"

Nice, huh?

I can take a lot. I've been with kids who got exorcisms. I saved a city from flying, fire-spitting gargoyles. And I won't even tell you why the Leaning Tower of Pisa is still leaning (now *that* was an assignment). But Rebecca? She was grating on my nerves faster than cheddar cheese melting in hot Texas chili.

I began to pray for my next assignment so I could get the heck out of Dodge. I willed a calling to come to me. That's when I get that feeling that a kid needs me. Then Throttle jet-sets me to my new master, who is always thirteen years old, like me.

Usually, I do not pray for assignments to come quickly. Not that I don't like my job, I love it. But the longer the breaks are between my assignments, the better. I love lounging around catching up on reruns of *The Simpsons*. And I adore lunching with my old wizard friends via crystal ball. Plus, I always need to catch up on my genie-mail. This time, I was three centuries behind on it because those younger genies are always genie-mailing me for wise advice. Believe me, I am *full* of advice — I've been a genie for more than a millennium.

What I needed to do, though, was inform the Genie Council that I captured Rebecca. I was procrastinating and not looking forward to that. The bigwigs up in France were not gonna be happy — not until I proved that she needed to be imprisoned for the rest of eternity. (Would I have to keep her and listen to her for that long? Oh my ponytail!) Luckily, I had some good reasons for capturing her. She broke the most basic rule of all genies: She was mean — and genies can never, ever, in a million trillion years, be mean. But the Genie Council would want to make it a long, drawn-out, formal process. The paperwork of the bureaucracy wears me out. But I won't wear you out talking about it.

"Genny! You are a stinking witch!" Rebecca screamed. "I HATE YOU!"

"Listen, blondie, you're the one who hasn't had a bath in a month," I retorted. "And baby cookie, I love you." I was just tormenting her. I threw a piece of pizza into her bottle. I may have disliked her an awful lot, but I wasn't about to starve her. She still griped — and griped and griped. I gave her a slice of my favorite food. Her screaming was making my brain throb.

And then it happened. Holy Hallelujah! Happy candied yams! I felt a calling coming on!

That meant I wouldn't have to hear the belly-aching or write my captured-genie report. Yippee!

As I prepared myself to leave Rebecca's House of Horrors, I said, "Throttle, please do something about that stench!" It really smelled like rotten peanut butter in there.

But horror of all horrors, the powers that be sent me to help a foreign creature.

They sent me to the aid of a . . . *boy*.

Ugh.

Chapter 3
"I've Got a Genie on My Mind"
by Andrew

She was such a cute girl, uh, genie. But more important than that, she was mine, all mine. All of my dreams (of MacKenzie) were going to come true! I was late to school because I was so happy about what I found in the millionaire's trash. I left the old computer parts there. I left the beautiful fabric that Gus would've wanted. I didn't even grab the old Tom Cruise movies that someone had pitched. I didn't care about any of that. This bottle and this genie inside were the only things in the world that made any difference to me. Finding her didn't make my day; it made my whole life.

She didn't say much while I escorted her back to my house. (I figured it would be a bad idea to take her with me to school.) In fact, the little paranormal chick didn't even really introduce herself. Instead, she looked kind of freaked out and worried. Normally, I would have thought her a bit rude — but something was obviously wrong, so I couldn't blame her for anything. As much as I wanted to cut class — which I would never, ever do (what if I missed doing a good homework assignment for someone?) — I had to get my tail end to homeroom. So I quickly tried to make her feel at home. I left her my warm, puffy sports stars sleeping bag. I brought her some Ovaltine and Soy Nuts. Even that didn't cheer her up! As a last-minute attempt at cheering her up in five seconds or less, I left her my Beatles CDs.

I was a little worried about her. But I'm going to admit something. And I hope it's not selfish to say this. Whether she was upset about something or not, I was still triple psyched to have my own genie. I left my banana-seat bicycle at home. I sprinted all the way to school just to burn off some nervous energy.

I didn't even freak out after arriving ten whole minutes late.

I walked into Modern Geography class and everyone giggled. So I stood in the doorway and inspected myself. Zipper up? Yep. Nose free of foreign totally gross objects? I thought so. Shoes on the correct feet? Yep. So why did they keep giggling? I didn't find out why until after fourth period. While washing my hands thoroughly with warm water and sudsy soap, I checked myself out in the mirror. My hair was standing straight up as if I had tried to put pieces of it in a mohawk. Obviously, I must've run my fingers through my hair when I still had peanut butter all over them. Result: Hair that was standing at perfect attention. I guess everyone thought this was especially funny because I (usually) have curly hair.

Why didn't anyone tell me? Well, after I thought and thought, I realized that it's because I was oblivious to everyone. All morning long, I had been in my very own little world. I couldn't get over the fact that I had my very own genie. This was amazing. A boy with a genie. *A teenage boy WITH A GENIE!!!* Do you remember what having a genie did for the guy in the Nick at Nite TV show? His life went from ho-hum to awesome! Mine was about to do the same, I knew it.

Not that I could complain about my life before my chance meeting with a genie. I have Gus — who may be a fashion designer, but he loves the Braves as much as I do — and Jane, who is the only person who can stay on the phone for fourteen hours at a time like I can. I also hang out with the cool dudes on the track team. Where, I admit it, I can smoke them all in the mile. I can run and run and run and run. I feel like I am in charge of the weather and the wind when I'm running. Plus, it makes me feel great to win — which I actually do a lot. I was built to run the mile.

I am also built to put together computers. No one had to teach me, I just started taking them apart and putting them back together when I was three. I learned it from watching a lot of infomercials. Sure, I can design Web sites and post them up. But what I really love to do is make new programs, mostly games that are way more hip than *Dungeons and Dragons*, but kind of like that. The guys on the football team always ask me to give them my new games.

The beefy jocks (I consider myself in the asparagus category of athletes) are all right. I have a lot of fun when we hang out together. But mostly I like them because they keep me in business. I can whip out A-plus homework, essays, book reports, and papers like nobody's beeswax. So I figured, it doesn't hurt to charge my schoolmates an arm and half of a leg for my services. They never complain — and I never let them down.

I use the money to buy the latest clothes and shoes. I mean, my parents buy me the basics like jeans and T-shirts. You know, I have the stuff I need. But Mom wants me to wear things that turn me into a total geek. So I usually pick out a few duds of my own. I think I am stylin', though Gus doesn't agree. He tells me I still look like a geek. Okay, maybe I don't match every single day. That's only because I'm totally color-blind. A guy can't help that, can he?

I wonder if a genie can do anything about my eyesight. I eat carrots four times a day, and that hasn't done a darn thing. At least my mom bought me some contacts. You should have seen me in my magnifying-lens glasses. I look much cooler now, if you ask me.

I thought about the genie all day. What was she doing? Did she find anything embarrassing in my bedroom? I knew I should have given my Snoopy stuffed toys away. And what if my parents saw her? What would I say? Surely they'd think I was up to no good if I told them, "Oh, she's just my live-in genie."

When school finally did let out, I ran home as fast as I could. And I can run pretty fast.

I just hoped she was in a better mood!

Chapter 4
"I'm Allergic to Boys!"
by Genny the Genie

What kind of assignment is this?

I think I'd rather go back in my bottle and listen to Rebecca scream at me. Put me with a boy? A member of the male kind? Shaving my head might be just as cruel. Did the Genie Powers That Be totally forget what it was like for me during the Civil War? I had four kid clients in a row who were born with Y chromosomes, and I nearly had a heart attack (except that genies are immune to major health problems). Modern boys just aren't like the ancient ones. Today's men are hyper and competitive — well, I guess guys always were that way. But the ones from this century? Most of them only think about sports and girls. They drive me absolutely batty. The thing is, while they may understand every single rule of football, they have no idea about what makes girls tick. The modern males I've been friends with think they can snap their fingers, and women will fall ponytail-deep in love with them just like that. Like wooing a woman is as easy as tossing a football! The biggest problem is, most guys don't bother to find out what chicks want and need. (So what if we are high-maintenance? That's beside the point.) Sorry to rant and rave, it's just that I understand Greek better than I understand guys. Wait a minute, I do know Greek. Oh, never mind.

I don't know why the Genie Powers That Be did this to me. They know my skills are best saved for members of my own gender.

I had to get myself together because, like it or not, there I was. Flags for some team called the Atlanta Braves were all over the place. He had all kinds of electronic music CDs. Every time I tried to listen to one, all I heard was BLIP BLIP, BUZZ BUZZ. That's not music! Oh, I missed Sophie playing her piccolo. Oh, I missed Nadia and her hip-hop. I wanted to listen to something with some soul! Thankfully, he did have a nice Beatles collection. I listened to "Michelle" about fifty times. That calmed me down. Until I was so rudely interrupted, as usual.

"YYYEEEEEOOOOOWWWW!" The scream was Rebecca's. How she tormented me and my kitty when we were out of the bottle, I don't know. I put a few pillows and the puffy sleeping bag over Throttle to muffle Rebecca's awful noises.

"DON'T THINK YOU'LL EVER BE ABLE TO ESCAPE ME. NEVER EVER EVER EVER! YEEEEEEEHAAAAAAAA!"

I was beginning to believe her. I don't know if she tormented me more when she was free and trying to kill me, or if I hated her more now, when she was my insanely, obnoxiously loud prisoner.

"ONE MILLION BOTTLES OF BEER ON THE WALL, ONE MILLION BOTTLES OF BEER. TAKE ONE DOWN, PASS IT AROUND, NINE HUNDRED AND NINETY-NINE THOUSAND, NINE HUNDRED, AND NINETY-NINE BOTTLES OF BEER ON THE WALL. NINE HUNDRED AND NINETY-NINE THOUSAND — "

I was going to wring my own neck just listening to her. Catfish dove into Andrew's closet to hide — then he jumped out because something in there scared him. Great — I didn't even want to think about what could be in there. Meanwhile, I frantically searched through his drawers and, fortunately, found some earmuffs to muffle Rebecca's awful singing.

I sat down on his bed and grabbed the stack of magazines sitting on his nightstand. *Runner's World, Running Today, Jogging for Teens* — that was his selection of fine reading material. Where were the teen fashion mags? Where were the Madonna CDs? Oh peasants pea!!! Things were not looking good for me.

"NINE HUNDRED AND NINETY-NINE THOU-SAND, NINE HUNDRED AND NINETY-TWO BOTTLES OF BEER ON THE WALL — "

I sat there in Andrew's earmuffs, tied my hair in knots, and tried not to cry.

Chapter 5

"The Way to a Genie's Heart"

by Andrew

"Hey there, what's the matter?" I asked this poor, pretty genie who was sitting on top of my Snoopy. She was a weird little thing. . . . She had my earmuffs on, and her cat was huddled way down deep in my dresser drawer. (I knew that only because a tail was hanging out and waving in the air.) I went over to my stereo and put on some Beatles music because that's usually soothing. I almost put on some techno to get her pumped up, but decided against it. It didn't matter what I played, though; the little genie just kept on crying.

"Is there anything I can do for you?"

She shook her earmuffs back and forth.

"Ah, come on," I said. "There has to be something that would make you feel better."

She looked at me, then put her head down

and cried some more. I wondered if maybe genies weren't all they were cracked up to be. Or maybe I got one who was malfunctioning. Aren't they supposed to bring fun and excitement to their masters' lives? Don't they tell jokes and make you smile? Mine wasn't doing any of that. In fact, my genie was far from chipper.

"Well, maybe you're hungry," I said. Food always cheers me up, anyway. "How about I treat you to some of my favorite snacks."

"I don't like Soy Nuts," she told me, sniffling. I forgot that I had given her some of those to snack on. No wonder she was crying! I wouldn't eat them, either — except that my mother makes me.

"Oh no, those aren't my favorite type of food. There's some pizza in the fridge."

"What kind?"

"Pepperoni."

I don't know what I had just done or said, but I definitely made some progress. She looked up and smiled.

"I would love some pepperoni pizza. By the way, my name is Genny."

Score! The pizza worked! I do have a way with the ladies.

I heated up a few slices for her and me. I didn't expect her cat to swipe one. Normally, I might have swiped it back. But I didn't want to cause any drama, especially now that she was starting to feel better. I made a mental note to always have some pizza on hand. Boy, I was psyched to see her mood improve. I had over three million questions to ask her.

"Why were you crying?" That was the first one.

"I don't know," she said. "Please just don't tell anyone. Genies aren't supposed to cry."

"I won't, I promise."

We sat there in silence for a few minutes. I noticed that being quiet around her was warm and easy, not at all awkward. Instantly she was like a high-maintenance best friend. I knew meeting her was meant to happen.

"You don't have to worry," she said. "I'm not always like this."

"Oh, like what?" I pretended not to have noticed her previous grumpiness.

"I've just had a long couple of days, that's all," she said.

"Believe me, I know what that's like."

"Just give me a few more minutes, and I'll be able to get down to business." With that, she disappeared into her bottle. I heard a lot of screaming, which made me a little antsy. Then I heard some rattling around. I crept closer to the bottle, putting my ear up against the opening. I heard some really terrible trash-talking. What was going on in there?

Poof!

Out Genny came, knocking me over. She had changed her clothes into a highly fashionable outfit that Gus would approve of. Along with fixing her hair, she had applied a shiny layer of lip gloss. The girl was pretty when she was wearing earmuffs and crying. But after a bit of fixing up, she was nothing other than gorgeous.

"Hmph!" she said as she sat down on my bed. "Spying on me, were you?" She grumbled something—I'm sure she had said, "Ugh. Men."

"I was, um, I was just worried. I heard lots of yelling in there, and I hoped you were okay. That's all."

"Well, I can manage that problem myself, but thanks for watching out for me, I guess."

"Yes, sure. I'm so sorry."

"Now, I'm going to give you the rules right now. I need you to sit down and listen."

"I'm all ears."

"Good. Anyway, I am not particularly thrilled about sharing a room with a boy. So, to ensure my own privacy, I will be staying in your closet. I expect you never to open it without knocking first."

"What if I need to get my clothes?"

23

"Don't worry about that. If you'd like me to, I'll lay your clothes out on your bed. Whatever you do, just don't go into the closet."

"Um, okay." I'm not sure I liked that arrangement. I tell you what, though, I didn't dare argue.

"The other rules are as follows: You are not to get dressed in my presence, because, as you may have noticed, you are a boy, and I am a girl. Please do it in the bathroom — and please don't come into this room wearing only a towel. That will freak me out. Okay, the second rule is that you must provide Q-Tips at all times."

"Huh?"

"Please, just do it. And never microwave my food. I don't like it like that."

"Okay." Who did this genie think she was? The princess of Nigeria?

"I like my diet Cokes cold but without ice. Bring them to me often. Buy some Madonna CDs and bring them to me immediately. And don't worry — your parents will not be able to hear or see me, although you may need to be quiet when you are talking. They can still hear what you are up to. You may reveal me to two friends if you want to. But if you show your genie to more people than that, I will disappear. So that's that. You have me for twenty-eight days, then I'm outta here. So what do you want? Oh, wait a minute. Do not ask me to make you a football star, war hero, or president of a small nation. I can't do any of that."

"Don't worry, I would never ask for such shallow things. Instead, I don't even have to think about it for a second. I know what I want."

"What?"

"I want this goddess of a girl named MacKenzie to fall madly in love with me. She goes to my school. And I've had a crush on her since before I was born. Can you make that happen?" When I said that, her stern face got softer. She didn't just smile at me; she was beaming.

"Is that really what you want?"

"Yes, if that's not against any of your rules or anything."

"Oh no, it's not. I love to help people solve their love problems. That's my specialty!"

Then she bounced over and hugged me. Things were definitely improving around here, even if I wasn't allowed to go into my closet. I asked her about all of the stuff I was dying to know. I found out that she was from France; that she had been on this earth for more than one thousand years; and that she goes around the world — mostly in America — helping thirteen-year-olds out of their pickles. She loves fashion and doesn't like sports, except she does enjoy playing coo-coo ball from time to time, whatever that is. I couldn't wait for her to meet Gus! They would have a lot to talk about. I was so glad that even though things were a mess in the beginning, she was turning out to be incredibly cool. She was bouncy, outgoing, hilarious, you name it! I knew I'd love having my own genie.

But there was something that was bugging me. "Genny, am I crazy, or is someone singing 'Bottles of Beer on the Wall'?"

"Oh that," she said, rolling her eyes. Then she handed me my earmuffs. "These are just about the only relief you're going to get. Unless I can think of a brilliant silencing spell, she'll just keep screeching."

"Wait, you do spells? Like magic?"

"Oh, honey! Just wait till you see me work my magic!"

Chapter 6
"Just Call Me Ms. Valentine!"
by Genny the Genie

Okay, maybe I was wrong. Andrew is not so bad. It's just that he didn't have any good magazines. And only a limited selection of decent music. Don't even get me started on his clothes. But he's got a killer personality — he and I just get along like chocolate chips and cookie dough. Overall, he is almost adorable, even if he is a boy. He's a tall, skinny kid with a brown curly mop for hair. He wears red shorts with orange shirts — so I'll make it my mission to improve this dude's style. Although to be completely honest, the quirky way he dresses fits him. He's got a few best friends he absolutely loves, who I'm supposed to meet when he gets home from school. A boy with best friends can't be all bad!

And he is totally in love with a girl named

MacKenzie. He told me that he's had a crush on her since they were in first grade. They used to be friends, but ever since they started junior high school, she hasn't given him two glances. Apparently, she is a very good skateboarder, and she spends all of her time with the alternative kids. So I asked him why he liked her. He told me that she was beautiful, inside and out. That was the sweetest thing I've ever heard from a teen! He likes the way she is so self-confident. In their classes, she always speaks her mind — and has very strong opinions. (She sounds like my kind of woman.) If someone is picking on someone else at school, she'll stand up for the underdog. He said she is conscientious and supersweet; she's even a candy striper at the hospital.

"The girl is a guy's dream come true," Andrew insisted last night.

I asked him if he's ever told *her* that, and he said, "Oh my gosh! Are you kidding? I would never say that to her."

So I pressed him on what he *has* talked to her about.

"Um, nothing."

"Does she know you like her?"

"The whole world knows how much I adore her."

"But wait, you mean you never talk to her?"

"I try to, but every time I see her, I get all quiet. I usually have a million words to say, like, all of the time — except when it comes to her. All I can mutter is hello, then I turn so red that I have to leave."

"You're kidding me!"

"It's embarrassing. And I'm *not* kidding you. But I do try to leave her all kinds of neat things next to her locker. Like jewelry, cute flower vases, and old tapes and records that I find."

"Does she know they're from you?"

"I don't know. I don't think so."

Oh boy — if she thinks a strange boy was leaving her gifts, the girl just might freak out. Leaving things for us girls is sweet, but, well, kind of weird. That conversation with Andrew definitely told me that he didn't get it when it came to MacKenzie. Yes, I was going to have quite an assignment ahead of me.

At least being in a boy's room wasn't going to be so bad. He had the coolest computer games I've ever played. I even got to play around in silence. Why? Because I put magic sleeping powder in Rebecca's food. Ahhh, Cat-fish and I were having the very best — most quiet — day in recent memory. Even Throttle looked more relaxed. The three of us took it easy, ate pizza, and truly enjoyed our day.

Before we knew it, Andrew showed up after school with two friends in tow.

I heard them coming up the steps and adjusted my ponytail. Ever so politely, Andrew tapped on his own bedroom door.

"Genny, it's me and my friends. Can we come in?"

"Of course!"

He introduced me to a well-dressed boy named Gus.

"Oh, man. Drew, I thought you were lying. Cool. Very cool," the boy said as he admired my outfit. "I love what you're wearing!" I told him thank you.

Next Andrew said, "This is Jane." She looked me up and down, smiled, then said, "Hello."

"Don't worry, I don't bite," I reassured her.

"I'm sorry. I've just never seen a genie before." Jane was very tall, and she looked like a total outdoorsy, tree-climbing type. She had dark Darth Vader–dyed hair. It was cropped way too short. But even with a bad haircut, the girl was just too cute.

I found out that Gus wants to be a fashion designer, and I just couldn't have been happier. He was too good to be true! In a million years, I wouldn't have guessed that I could have so much in common with a boy. We talked on and on for almost an hour. He loved hearing all about me and the designer Vera. I taught her everything she knew back when she was just thirteen! Gus was so fascinated. He even knew who she was! I showed him my Vera collection, which included five of her funky, colorful dresses and tons more sixties-style shirts.

Andrew and Jane were totally into it! Then I told Jane I had worked with Jacques Cousteau. She really loved hearing about him because she loves the wildlife in the ocean. When Andrew left the room, I told Gus and Jane a big-time secret. See, all of my kid masters, like Andrew, become famous one day. Don't ask me why; I don't know. But every single kid I've ever helped goes on to do great things. I usually don't know what or when, but it always happens. They were so thrilled to hear that. I made them swear that they wouldn't tell Andrew that secret until I left. They promised to zip their lips.

Andrew came back to his room and sat on the bed. I noticed that Jane sat cuddly-close to him. She put her hands on his shoulders a lot, and then I saw him slowly inch away. I wondered if he was crazy — the girl was amazing! I told Catfish to remind me to get the scoop later. He bit me — his way of telling me to mind my business. As if!

The three kids talked and talked. Andrew said

he needed to write a book report for a guy at school. But before the kids left, I overheard an interesting conversation, one that reinforced my ancient belief: Sometimes things are just meant to be.

"Did you hear that everyone has a date to the eighth-grade dance already?" Jane asked.

"No way, there's still time to get a date," Andrew said.

"Well, you better hurry! Or everyone will pair off, and we'll have to go by ourselves!"

Gus and Andrew did look a little worried.

This assignment couldn't be more up my dark and windy alley. Just call me Cupid — I have a love plan up my ponytail!

Chapter 7
"I'm Not the Romeo I Want to Be!"
by Andrew

I couldn't believe what Jane said! Everyone already has dates for the dance? And it's only three weeks away? I could have sworn that I had more time left than that. This news equals disaster. I might as well flunk a test! I thought I had plenty of time to ask MacKenzie to that dance. I have been dreaming about taking her to it — the biggest shindig of our lives (hey, we're three years away from the prom!) — for most of my existence. I would trade all of the cool stuff I ever found; I would give away all of my computer equipment; I would even stop running the mile.

I hope my genie can help me! It's weird that she showed up just in time. I think she knows more about me than I do, even though we just met.

I really wanted her to stay up all night so we could start making a plan. Anyone could see that I needed a supernatural formula so MacKenzie will want to talk to me. I shake all over whenever that girl is within ten feet of me. I stutter and trip over things. I make such a dork of myself that even my closest friends can't help but laugh at me. See, I may be able to run fast, fix computers, and get A-pluses on assignments, but when it comes to that girl MacKenzie, all of a sudden I'm a geeky loser. Why can't I just be myself with her like I am with my best friend Jane?

Well, I used to be totally at ease with my best friend Jane. But she's been acting a little weird lately. I don't know why — we've been the best of friends since the first grade. We were always on the same accelerated reading teams. She, Gus, and I could talk for hours — we had every-thing in common. (Well, except that Gus was much better at art and drawing than he was at computers and competitions.) Anyway, what I was trying to tell you is that I was glad Jane went home — and not just because I had to fin-ish up that book report.

Jane knows that I'm not dumb. I noticed when she sat too close to me. I caught her touching my shoulders a little too much. I see the way she looks at me. I don't think I like it at all. Let me try to explain. Would you like it if you got a love letter from your cousin? I don't think so. Well, I didn't like getting a romance vibe from Jane.

Of course, Genny noticed Jane's behavior, too. She waited patiently for me to finish up the report — she was busy singing Madonna songs and dancing with her cat. They were a bit goofy, but it's not like I mind. Then those two played Rummy 500. Finally, when I was done, Genny lit into me.

"So, I really like Jane," she said.

"Uh, yeah, me too. But I want to talk to you about that dance. You have to help me! I have to go with MacKenzie!"

"Oh, MacKenzie, shapenzie. Jane is the most beautiful girl I've ever seen."

I never look at her that way! What was Genny talking about? "Um, you think so?" I didn't want to be mean. I guess I know she could be pretty. But I just don't like to think about that. "Okay, so did you hear what she said about that dance?"

"Oh yes," she said, sounding like she was up to something. "I heard what she said."

I was preparing to tell her there was no way that I could go to something like that with Jane.

I wanted Genny to get that idea out of her head right away. Wasn't she there to help me win over MacKenzie? I was just about to ask her. Then, of course, the phone rang.

"Hello," I said. Who would be on the other line? What kind of luck would I have? "Oh, hi, Jane." That's what kind.

She just beat around the bush and talked about Gus and school. Gus was all excited about starting a club called FFD, Future Fashion Designers. Jane thought that was just too cool. All the girls at school thought so, too. They all loved Gus; he made girls cool shirts and skirts. (He is such a huge flirt!) But why was Jane discussing this with me? We'd talked about it twenty times already. I knew there was something else going on.

Oh boy, I found out. I got off the phone and said, "Oh, Genny! HELP ME! What am I going to do?"

"What, Andrew? Who was that?"

"It was Jane! Do you know what she wanted? *Do you!!!???*"

"What? What?"

"She asked me to the dance! The eighth-grade dance! Can you believe that?"

"Well, yeah, she was totally flirting with you tonight. I'm not surprised. I think it's really cute!"

"Aren't you here to help me get MacKenzie?"

"Yes, but Jane is so great. What did you tell her?"

"I didn't say anything. I said I had to go, and that we would talk about it tomorrow. What a mess! She knows how much I like MacKenzie. But of course I don't want to hurt her. She's my best friend. What am I going to do?"

Genny just shook her head. She was kind of smiling, which I didn't like one bit.

"You're my genie, and I need your help! Please tell me what to do."

"Don't worry, don't worry," she said, trying to calm me down. "Andrew, sweet pea, I will help you get through this."

"But Jane said she loved me!"

Chapter 8
"I Am Sneaky – and Really Smart!"
by Genny the Genie

Talk about a pickle. This boy is in one. If only he would fall madly in love with that sweet girl Jane. As far as I could tell, they'd go together like a mouse and cheese, ketchup and french fries, or the beach and a romantic Florida sunset. If only he could see in her what I saw in her . . .

She and I hit it off. We were kindred spirits, kind of like me and my best friend, Laurie, back in old France. Oh, how I miss her. She had the worst hair of anyone you ever met, just like Jane does. But you couldn't find a better peasant to hang out with. She was the bichon frise of friends. I bet Jane is an amazing friend, too.

Gus and I discussed Jane in depth. He faked a high temperature and stayed home from school. He had some clothes to make, but he needed some time to get them done. He knew I was sitting at Andrew's all alone, so he brought them over. I bet I surprised him when he saw that I could design and sew every bit as great as he can! Anyway, we had a really good talk. I guess I shouldn't be so hard on boys. Some of them — like Gus and Andrew — are surprisingly sweet and sensitive.

Gus has red hair — much brighter than mine — and lots of freckles. He is supercute. He's so not what you'd think of in a clothing designer. He's pudgy and stocky — built like a spear-thrower or wrestler. He's superfriendly and flirty. But he isn't so good at keeping secrets. He told me all about Jane's crush on Andrew, even though she pinky-swore him to keep his mouth shut.

"It all started about a year ago," Gus said. "Andrew brought Jane a fishing net, then took her to the pier. Something about the sunset, the water, and the waves did a number on her. Ever since then, she can't get him out of her head. It's really strange. Actually, I don't like it one bit."

"Why? Are you jealous?"

"Me? No, not me. Uh, why would I be jealous? It's just that we're friends and once we start going out with each other what we have will be ruined."

"Or maybe your bond will become even stronger."

"I don't know. I am just tired of hearing Jane go on and on and on about it."

I could tell that was a sore subject, so I changed it. "Tell me about MacKenzie."

"She's just this dumb girl. I don't know what he sees in her. To be honest, I don't even like her."

"You don't? Why?"

"For one, she's not nice to Andrew. Everyone in five school districts knows Andrew Green is in love with MacKenzie Brown. You'd think she could at least be nice to him."

"IS she mean?"

"Kinda. She doesn't say a word to him. He'll say hello, and she'll just walk right off."

"Really? That's so terrible! What kind of girl would do that?"

"A girl who thinks she's pure gold. Wait a minute — more than that. MacKenzie thinks she's made of platinum. She rides around on her skateboard fiddling with her long hair. Actually, her hair is a lot like yours. But she — I don't know — she flaunts it. She knows it looks good or something. She giggles to all of her skater friends and just acts like she's so smart and awesome. Blah. I don't know what he sees in her. To be honest, he'd be better off with Jane. She is an awesome girl."

"My job, as you may well know, is to get MacKenzie to like Andrew. Not only that, Andrew wants her to go to the dance with him. Is there any possibility of that happening?"

"No. She hasn't talked to him since the first grade, when she used to borrow his crayons."

"That's what I needed to know."

I had to try Plan B, whether Andrew liked it or not. While Gus was there, I reached into my bottle and pulled out my tape recorder. I turned it on and said to Gus, "So, Jane wants to go to the dance with Andrew."

"I don't want Jane to take Andrew."

"Would you go with her?"

"Sure I would . . . I'd go with Jane. I mean, I wish the three of us could go together."

"Well, would you ever consider going with me? I mean, just as friends."

"Sure, that'd be fun, I'd love to go to the dance with you, too." Just as Gus said that, I turned off the tape recorder. I had just what I needed. Catfish — who is especially smart when he's chewing his Q-Tips — figured out what I was up to.

When Gus left, I spliced the tape so that it said, "Sure, Jane. I'd love to go to the dance with you."

I called up Jane's house and played it on her answering machine. After all, Gus and Andrew sound a whole lot alike. So she'd think Andrew was answering her big question from last night. Now the hard part was coming. I had to convince Andrew, somehow, that he liked Jane . . . and not this mean, spiteful, hateful MacKenzie girl. How dare she be wicked to my Andrew!

Chapter 9
"We Talked Trash"
by Genny the Genie

Andrew came home all upset about this MacKenzie thing. My stomach was falling down into my ankles. That's how worried I was that I'd done the right thing.

"I guess I have to call Jane," he said. "I have to tell her the truth . . . that I don't want to go with her. She's my best friend; I owe her that, don't I?"

"You can't call her," I snapped.

"Why? What's going on?"

"Um, she's not home tonight. Gus was here this afternoon, and he said Jane had to go to dinner with her parents."

"Eat out? Her parents are gourmet chefs. They never eat out."

"But they had to tonight. It was some special something or other."

"Well, all right. Maybe she didn't have a

chance to tell me about it because I avoided her all day. I'll just call her later."

I had to make him forget about later. So we went junk collecting out in the mansions' garbage alleyways. I couldn't believe how cool it was! Andrew let me ride in the basket of his banana-seat bike. He told me all about himself and his family. He is an only child whom his parents adore. It's just that they're always too busy working to hang out with him. He talked about school. I was sad when he told me that secretly he's always felt like an outsider even though most kids are nice to him. "I'm just not like anyone else," he told me.

"Then you aren't boring. You are unique, Andrew. You are a very special boy."

"You think so?" he said as he rummaged through a box of old jewelry. "Ah, this is sterling silver! You want this, Genny?" I had to admit, the ruby earring was cool, even if there was only one of them.

I put it into my third earhole and said, "I know how great you are. You want to hear a secret?"

"Lay it on me."

"I didn't want to be put with a boy. That's why I was crying when I met you."

"Why not?"

"I thought all boys were bloodthirsty heathens. I thought all they cared about was sports. But you . . . You don't kill bugs or smash things against your head. You don't even talk about running very much."

"Oh, I think about running. But not too much, it's too easy. I'm more interested in the challenging aspects of my life."

"That's why I like you. You're different."

He reached deeper into the trash can and fished around some more. He found the other sterling silver ruby earring. He held my hand and said, "This is for you."

Chapter 10
"Was There Life Before Genny?"
by Andrew

I've been having a blast with my genie! She's the coolest female I've ever met. She loves all things girlie, but she doesn't get on my nerves. It's the weirdest thing. We talk and have fun. I'm even getting her to appreciate electronic music. She hated it when she got here a whole week ago. Now I think she actually digs it! At least, once I showed her how you're supposed to dance to it — you know, just hop around a lot — she really enjoyed it. She asked me to put it on and danced with me for three nights in a row.

Of course, she also showed me how to dance to other kinds of music. I have to admit it, I'm not a very good dancer. I usually thwack people in the head when hip-hop comes on. So Genny put on the rap station and showed me how to bounce around. When she was done with me, I looked like a genuine soul man. She helped me out with my mosh-pit moves, too. Now I just jump straight up and down and move my hips. Oh, and did I tell you I can almost waltz now? Genny told me that was a sure way to woo the women. "If you can waltz at the eighth-grade dance, girls will think you're sweet and sensitive," she said. She and I waltzed and waltzed and waltzed. It was pure heaven.

Bonding with her wasn't like hanging out with other girls. I didn't feel nervous around her like I did with MacKenzie. And I didn't get the romance heebie-jeebies when I was with Genny like I did when I was with Jane. Speaking of her . . . I don't know why she's being so nice lately. But wow, she is. I wrote her a big, long letter about how we were better off as friends. I slipped it into her locker and *voilà* (Genny taught me that word) everything seemed back to normal again.

Meanwhile, Genny keeps telling me that she's teaching me everything that will help me be the perfect boy. I told her I just wanted to ask MacKenzie to the dance, but she insisted that it's not that easy. "You have to know what makes us tick, Andrew. After spending one thousand and thirteen years with a girl — myself — I think I know what we want."

She could teach me anything she wanted for as long as she wanted. That's how much fun Genny and I were having together. The days at school were extra long because I couldn't wait to get home and see her. I was learning that much! I have to admit, I stopped doing other kids' homework assignments for a while because they take up so much of my time. And I had only three more weeks to spend with my genie. I figured I could go back into business then.

It's when I was busy thinking about Genny — we were going to watch chick flicks when I got home — that I bumped into MacKenzie. I was walking down the hall, looking at the ground. I turned the corner to go into literature class and *boom*! MacKenzie was just coming out. My first thought was, *Oh my . . . she is beautiful.* It's my second thought that surprised me. This went through my head: *So what if she's gorgeous? Genny is, too, and if I have to be honest, so is Jane. Who cares?* I said hello to her without stuttering once. I really didn't even feel that nervous.

"Hi," she said.

I didn't want to blow my one shining moment to say something intelligent back to her. So since she was just leaving the class that I had next, I said, "So, how dull was English today?"

"Oh my gosh! It was so boring. You wouldn't believe how Mrs. Smithford can go on for an hour about the ending *-ly*. It was murder staying awake."

I actually like talking about *-lys* and the other things that are useless in our English language, but I wasn't about to tell MacKenzie that. "Yeah, that sounds awful. Let me know if you ever need help with your homework."

"Um, okay," she said as she walked away.

I strolled into class, feeling about fifty feet tall instead of five-ten. It was a great feeling. I just had my first normal, intelligent conversation with MacKenzie Brown.

Chapter 11
"You Did What?"
by Andrew

I rushed home to hang with Genny. I didn't want to go to track practice, so I skipped it. I didn't even stop to check out the rich people's trash. I hadn't decided whether to tell Genny about what had happened with MacKenzie.

As soon as I burst into my bedroom, Genny was standing there waiting for me. "Listen," she said. "Sit down."

"What's going on?"

"Don't be mad at me, okay?"

"Why would I be mad at you?"

"Jane just called, and she's on her way over."

"What?" Jane hadn't been over in several days — which was weird, because we used to spend so much time together. Actually, when I stopped to think about it, Gus hadn't been over for a millennium, either. "That's good, I guess I need to talk to her." I hadn't chatted with Jane since I left her my "let's just be friends" letter. But I needed to do it. I didn't want us to avoid each other forever.

"One more thing," Genny said.

"Yeah."

"She's coming here to talk about the dance."

"What *about* the dance?"

"Um, well, she thinks she's going with you."

"WHAT? What are you talking about? Did you microwave some food that you're allergic to?"

"It's a long story, Andrew. Please don't get mad. You've just got to go with her."

"But — I didn't tell you this — I had my first real conversation with MacKenzie today. I mean, I'm making progress with her! I thought you were here to help me with *her*!"

"Uh-oh."

"How did this happen? How come Jane thinks I'm going with her? I know, Gus told her. That Gus . . . I'm calling him right this second."

"No, don't! Gus didn't have anything to do with it! I did!"

"Oh no . . . What did you do? I did *not* ask you to set me up with Jane!!!"

"To make a long story short, *I* kinda-sorta took it totally upon myself to, um, well, tell her you'd go with her."

51

"Well, I am *not* happy. . . . But I'm still okay, because I just wrote her a letter saying how she and I were better off as friends."

"Um, well . . ."

"WHAT? Oh no!" I screamed.

"She never got your letter."

"Yes, she did, I put it in her locker myself."

"No, um, well. I saw your letter on your back-pack, and I replaced it with a blank piece of paper. So, um, you gave Jane a — "

"A blank piece of paper?!!! Genny, what are you trying to do to me? The only thing I asked you to do was help me go to the dance with MacKenzie. That is the only thing I wanted. I didn't ask for fame, fortune, or much of anything!"

"You're right, and I truly am so sorry. I talked to Gus, though, and he didn't like MacKenzie very much. And, well, I really love Jane. I did it because I didn't want to help get you together with a jerk. I did it because I want you to be happy, and I thought you'd be happiest with Jane."

"Genny, MacKenzie is not a jerk. Gus doesn't even know her. He just doesn't want any of us to pair up! He's so afraid of anything messing up our friendship. Can't you see that? I knew he was involved somehow!"

"Oh, really? But I'm telling you, it's got noth-

52

ing to do with him. I don't even think he wants you to be with Jane. . . . There's another reason I did this," Genny said. "And I'm sorry, but I have to be honest . . . I didn't think MacKenzie would go with you."

"You didn't think she would? Why? Am I that much of a dork?"

"No, no. You're wonderful! Gus just told me that — "

"I can't wait to give Gus an earful. And what am I supposed to do about Jane? I'd rather go to the dance with a potato sack than go with Jane!"

"Don't say that," Genny said.

"Why? It's true. Dating Jane? That's sounds about as much fun as breaking my big toe on purpose."

"Be quiet, Andrew, she could be here any second."

"Going with her would be as romantic as going with my grandmother."

Just then, we heard someone stomping down the stairs. I looked out my window and soon saw Jane running down the street. Oh, boy, had I done it this time. I would have done anything to take those words back. The last thing I wanted to do was hurt Jane. I swear, I didn't mean those nasty things! I was just trying to make Genny understand how I felt! "Now what am I supposed to do?" I swear, I swear, I didn't mean to blow Jane's feelings into little bitty bits!

"This is not good," Genny said.

"This is *definitely* not good," I agreed.

Chapter 12
"My Intentions Were Good!"

by Genny the Genie

Everything was going a little haywire. For one thing, I ran out of magic sleeping powder and Rebecca began screaming again. Lucky for me, I didn't have to go into my bottle all that much since I was having such a great time with Andrew. But still, we could all hear her from his bedroom. There was no escaping the crazy, evil witch. After the latest fiasco, Rebecca started cackling.

"HA-HA-HA-HA-HA-HA-HA-HA! You stupid, clumsy genie. You should get your ponytail removed painfully and slowly for that one. Hair by ratty hair!"

She was also in a tirade because she had missed so much of the action in this assignment. By this time — a week since I met Andrew — she had figured out my magic sleeping dust trick. Of course, that did not make her one bit happy. Not that she was ever happy to begin with.

"I'll never eat again! Not if you're going to poison me! I'll starve. I'll die in here. What will the Genie Council think of you then? You are a MEAN, EVIL genie! MEAN MEAN MEAN MEAN!!!"

Really, that was the one insult that hurt me most. I was not mean — although I may have accidentally been mean to Jane and Andrew. I put on Andrew's earmuffs and tried to ignore her. Meanwhile, Andrew was sitting on his bed trying to ignore me.

"I'm really sorry. I'll tell Jane it's all my fault. I'll help you get MacKenzie. We still have two whole weeks before the dance. We have plenty of time to woo her. You're really amazing, Andrew. You have to believe that, and you can have any girl you want."

"You think so?" he said. "I don't know. Right now, I feel like a terrible person. I can't believe what I've just done to Jane. You have to help me make it up to her."

"I can definitely do that. I got you into it — I can get you out." I just hoped I could keep that promise. I would think of something, right?

"Genny, you are a wicked witch!" The too-familiar screech came roaring from the background. At that moment, I did not need to hear those words. Catfish started meowing. Usually a cat's whines are unbearable, but Andrew and I liked them — at least when he was meowing, we couldn't hear Rebecca from Texas. I went into Throttle for a few minutes to desperately search for some magic sleeping dust. I had no luck. I put piles of clothes on top of her tiny bottle inside my bottle to muffle the noise a bit.

I popped back out of the bottle, and Andrew was on the phone. He was talking to Gus about what had just happened. I could hear in his voice that he was annoyed with his friend: Really, even if Andrew didn't believe me, this whole mess had nothing to do with Gus.

I eavesdropped intently on Andrew's conversation.

"You want me to help you start the Future Fashion Designers? Why?"

It didn't sound like it was going so well.

"Well, Gus, I can't. I'm too busy with Genny and track and homework assignments. Besides, I'm color-blind. I can't even match my clothes."

"I know you'll help me," Andrew said after a pause. "It's just that, well, I don't give a cat's meow about fashion."

There was silence, except for Catfish's whining — he really didn't like that comment.

"Come on, Gus, you know I didn't mean it

that way. . . . Yeah, well, you've been acting weird, too. Why are you always taking Jane's side of things?"

Uh-oh. Andrew was in deep enough — I sure hoped he wasn't duking it out on the phone with Gus.

"Fine, then. 'Bye." Andrew slammed the phone down and looked at me. I thought he'd be peeved at me for starting all of this mess. But he was mad at mostly Gus. Andrew was hoppin' furious.

"Why isn't Gus helping me out? I didn't mean to do that to Jane. I tried to tell him that I didn't leave her a phone message saying I would go. I guess you did that, didn't you, Genny?"

"Um, well — "

"It doesn't matter who did what now. The damage is already done. And today, of all days, Gus has to tell me to join the FFD."

"I love the FFD."

"Genny! I can't help him with that, and he knows it. I don't like to dress up, but besides that, I couldn't care less about fashion. And you know what?"

"What?"

"I even told him so."

"Oh no." Andrew was doing this weird one-eighty while I was around. He was still fun and cool and quirky. But he definitely wasn't his usual self. He had stopped spending time doing the things he used to do — all he did was hang out in his room. He also wasn't being as nice as he could be to Gus or Jane. I thought hard about what was going on with him. I only came to one conclusion: He's a boy, and as much as I may try, I still don't quite understand him.

Chapter 13
"This Is How Things Are Now"
by Andrew

Nothing is going my way.

Gus is out-of-his-mind mad at me. He didn't really say it, but I think it's about Jane. He doesn't want me to hurt her — and I don't want to hurt her, either. Gus just doesn't understand that I didn't mean to do anything I did. Or maybe he's really mad because I haven't joined his club. I'm not sure why he would care — we don't have to do *everything* together. It's not like he rummages through the trash with me. Although he *does* go to my home track meets. I try to do other nice things for him, like bringing him free cool material and fixing his computer when it crashes. Oh darn, I don't know what to do. My friends and I never fight. In fact, we haven't had a spat since we were in the third grade, and Jane hung out with two other boys instead of hanging out with us. She came to her senses and came back to us, so that one worked itself out. This situation was going to take a little more work! It was so ambiguous. Jane, my practical ocean-loving friend, had lost her mind. Why did she like me? She was way too serious, smart, and organized for me. I can be quite a handful to keep up with — I always have three million things going on. And Gus, oh Gus! He is so popular with the girls — they'll all be waiting in line to join his club. Why did he give an embroidery thread about me?

How did everything get so messed up?

If I really stop and think about it, life was going smoothly until I met Genny. But the thing is, I love having her here with me. She is unlike anyone I've ever met before. Stuff she says makes me laugh — and her stories fascinate me. You should hear about some of the way-famous people she's met. And some of the things she's done! She's jumped out of burning buildings; she's told off kings who were famous for cutting off people's heads; she's stared down fire-breathing dragons. Looking at her, you wouldn't think she was brave. But don't be fooled — this genie is not afraid of anything.

She and I can talk all night long and still not be tired of each other. Hanging around with her makes me happy. So it doesn't matter if she isn't, well, doing the things I asked her to. Sure, going to the dance with MacKenzie would be nice, but it isn't so important anymore.

As for wrecking things between me and Jane, I don't know how Genny did it. But I can't be mad at either of them . . . Jane's crush on me was going to blow up in our faces at some point anyway. But if I had handled it the way I wanted to, without Genny involved, there would have been a lot less hurt. I do hope Genny is more skilled at getting me out of this than she was at getting me into it. She may be able to tackle ancient world problems — but what about me and my friends' fights? It's so weird because, like I said, we *never* fight.

I have to admit something — I don't care whether Genny is around for the sole purpose of solving my problems or not. I just want her around. Fortunately, she hasn't left me alone for two days, since the whole Jane thing happened. She has been working hard to smooth things over. For example, she called Jane and did the apologizing for me. Jane just got mad, though, and said I should be calling her. So that's what I did — I called her to try to apologize. I couldn't — she wouldn't take my calls. I can't win! I miss her as my friend — I hope that's what Jane and I are again someday: two really close friends. But I certainly don't blame her for being upset — I would be hurt if someone said they'd rather date their granny than go out with me, too. And Gus . . . I hope things aren't weird between us for much longer. It's not like we're not talking. He's cool at school, and we talk on the phone. But he is being distant toward me.

Genny says she's thinking of a plan to get the three of us back together. In the meantime, she's determined to teach me to woo MacKenzie. Although it doesn't matter as much as it used to, I have to say that I was doing pretty well on my own lately. I see her coming out of English class every day now, and we stop and chat. I don't stutter and stumble around anymore, probably because I'm just not nervous. It's miraculous! Why am I all of a sudden not a mess in her presence? MacKenzie has told me about the new skateboarding moves she just mastered. And she seems really interested to see me run the mile at a meet. I mean, ever since I stopped thinking about her and worshipping her twenty-four hours a day, I'm finally — after nearly seven years — getting somewhere. How strange is that?

Genny has been coaching me on what to say and how to act. Since she's a girl and I'm not, I really have to trust her on this. Like, she told me that I should never seem too eager to talk to any girl. "We like it when you're nice to us," she explained. "But if you are too sugary, complimentary, and mushy, then we just think you're up to something. We think you're trying to trick us into going out with you — or even worse, if you're too sweet, we'll wonder if you've got any spark to your personality. Andrew, girls really do like spark. We also love it when a guy acts normal around us. You know, Andrew, like how you act around me."

She was right. I was totally comfortable with her . . . well, most of the time. The past few days, she's been giving me butterflies, and I don't know why.

She kept on coaching me, not noticing the way I watched her. "You have to start keeping a list in your pocket. In fact, I'll help you make it right now. Got a pen and a paper?"

I asked her, "What kind of list are you talking about?"

She said, "An Andrew-Is-All-That List. You need to be more confident around girls, especially MacKenzie. You've been such a 'fraidy cat in front of her before — no wonder she wasn't totally attracted to you. If you continue to act calm, cool, and confident, things will be different, I promise. So anyway, what I want you to do is this: Write down the things that you are great at — and I don't just mean running, fiddling with computers, and acing homework assignments. Write down some of your other awesome qualities."

"I can't think of any."

"I can . . . I'll start them out for you. Number one: You're extremely open-minded — you don't judge anyone. Your motto seems to be: Everyone is cool until they prove themselves otherwise."

"I guess that's true."

"Two, you are yourself. You don't care what everyone else is doing or what is cool at the moment. You are very independent and original."

"Oh, stop," I said. I did want her to go on, though.

"Three, you are adorably handsome, and don't you forget it."

I blushed. I almost told her how gorgeous she was, but I bit my lip.

"Four — are you writing all of this down? — good. Then four, Andrew is well liked by lots of people. Do you know anyone who dislikes you?"

"Jane."

"She doesn't count — she loves you while she hates you."

"Oh, great."

"Anyway, there's a reason everyone digs

you — you've got a great personality. You make people smile, and you usually go out of your way to keep things calm. Although you did tell Gus you didn't want to be in the FFD."

"Ugh. Was that really bad?"

She went down the rest of her Andrew-Is-Awesome list. She said, "Five, you're one of the sweetest guys I've ever met. Six, you are brave to pick through other people's garbage a couple of times every day. Seven, you're generous because you garbage-pick so you can give cool stuff to your parents and friends. Eight, you're smart and enterprising because you sell stuff you find on-line. Oh, and you have a homework business going on here — that's pretty brilliant of you, too. Although I do think you should just be helping your friends with their assignments instead of doing all of the work for them. Anyway, number nine: You're totally reliable — you're always on time. Ten: You're you."

She made me put the list in my pocket, then she hugged me. I started to feel *very* nervous. I wasn't totally sure why . . . but I had an idea.

Chapter 14
"My Heart-to-Heart With a Future Fashion Designer"
by Genny the Genie

A few days have gone by, and Andrew's had that list with him at all times. I can't believe how well it's working. He and MacKenzie even sat together at lunch today! That is a sure sign that things around here are looking up. All he had to do was force himself to talk to her and not be nervous. Reminding him how cool he was really did the trick. I don't know if she likes him in a girlfriend kind of way. I do know that they are becoming friends. That's a great thing!

Gus came over when Andrew was at track practice. I'm helping him start the FFD club. We made all kinds of patterns for beginners. There are a bunch of kids who want to join but don't know how to sew. Gus is happy to teach them what to do.

"Genny, what do you do when someone has a crush on you?" he said.

"That depends on who it is. Do tell, Gus, who's got it bad for you?"

"I can't say this to anyone but you. . . . Please don't tell Jane or Andrew."

"I would never!" I was twisting my ponytail into tight knots, I wanted to know the scoop so bad!

"I think a couple of girls at school are only joining my club because they like me."

"You're kidding! Why do you think that?"

"I don't know. I just get a love vibe. They call me all the time, and they stop by. It's getting out of hand! To tell you the truth, that's why I wanted Andrew to join me so badly. I know he hates fashion, but I just don't think I can handle all of these women by myself!"

I had to hold back my laugh — I looked down to hide my smile. Catfish was rolling around on the ground, holding his belly. Gus was all the rage with the girls! So cute! I composed myself before I asked, "Do you like any of them back?"

"I like them all," he said. "Just not romantically."

"Oh, kinda like how Andrew feels about Jane."

"Yes . . . exactly. So what do I do? I can't let them think that I like them. But I want them to stay in my club."

"Listen, they like what you do — and they like who you are. They won't quit the club just because you don't feel all mushy about any of them. You just need to be gentle. Next time you're hanging out with your female friends, just mention that you are madly in love with someone from Texas! That's a good way to let them down easy. You're telling them that your heart is already taken."

"I don't want to be mean to them!"

"No, not mean. Just try to be less desirable. Gus, you dress really well — girls love that. Plus, you're cool. You better get used to girls liking you. So anyway, around these girls, scratch your armpits and burp a bit. That's a good way to get them to stop liking you."

"What a great idea! I'll try that tomorrow."

I asked Gus for the scoop on Andrew. I told him I wanted everyone to kiss and make up. Gus said that Jane was still out-of-her-mind sad over what Andrew had said about her. I can't tell you how bad that news makes me feel. I truly feel like it's all my fault. I just don't know how to make things better. Gus says he's been spending a lot of time with her, trying to console her. He said Andrew has been a jerk. All he does is spend every waking second with me. Or talking about me. That was weird — but I told Gus not to worry. I'd have to leave in two weeks anyway.

"He's changing, Genny. He doesn't pick through trash anymore; he doesn't go to track practice every day; he doesn't even work on his computers. I don't feel like I know him as well as I used to. Even at school he's not the same. If you can believe this — he's always talking to MacKenzie."

That was a shocker. He told me things were going better — but I didn't know they were actually hanging out. "You're kidding! Why didn't he tell me that?"

"You don't know, Genny?"

I looked at Gus, very puzzled. It made no sense. It seems like my own kid master would be bursting to tell me that my perfect-boy plan was working for him. I didn't get it at all. "Is there something you're not telling me?"

"No, no. Just forget it. Anyway, I told you, MacKenzie just isn't my favorite girl."

Andrew said she was supercool. So I said to Gus, "Tell me the truth . . . . Is she *really* that bad? I can't believe Andrew would like a jerk."

He was silent for a minute. I did a truth chant in my head, hoping that would make him tell me what was really going on. Lots of things were fishy. "Tell me, please."

"She isn't that bad. I'm just afraid that Andrew will leave us for her. I can't stand the thought of Jane, Andrew, and me ever breaking up." He began to sway back and forth, looking at his feet. He looked as if a beloved pet just died. Oh my!

That was so sad! At least a few things were starting to make a bit more sense. Gus just wanted things to stay the same — he didn't want their childhood friendship to change! Oh, poor Gus. Things can't help but keep changing.

Chapter 15
"I Ran for My Love Life!"
by Andrew

I cannot believe that girl! Jane is being im-pos-sible. She won't talk to me, even though I've been trying to tell her I'm sorry for a whole week. And today . . . I swear, she is going to drive me nuts. This just isn't like her!

I was talking to MacKenzie at lunch. I've been sitting with her because Gus is still acting weird, and anyway, he sits with Jane, who isn't speaking to me. Who else am I supposed to sit with? Besides, MacKenzie and I have a lot in common. She likes computers as much as I do. I also like the way she does stuff for other people. You can tell by the way she talks that she loves being a candy striper at the hospital. She has made friends with all of the old dying people. Now I know for sure why I liked her for all of those years — the girl is about as cool as they come. Genny is, too, but I won't get started on her right now.

So back to what Jane did today . . . I was sitting with MacKenzie when Jane sat down behind me. She started talking really loudly to a guy we have class with. (Gus wasn't there yet.) She yelled, "Ohhh! Yikes! A roach! Eeek! Andrew, I told you to clean out your moldy backpack." Everyone looked at me in disgust. MacKenzie looked at me, horrified. I knew if I defended myself to the whole lunchroom, everyone would just laugh. So I said quietly to MacKenzie, "Jane is mad at me, that's why she said that." MacKenzie seemed super-relieved to hear that there weren't really roaches living in my book bag.

I could have killed Jane. I went home fuming. Genny told me to forget about it. "Just let her get it out of her system. When she feels like she's gotten you back, then maybe she can finally forgive you."

"I hope so . . . but she's going to make me seem like this really gross geek before she's finished. Not that I mind being a dork . . . but I *do* mind it if people think I'm a dirty, roach-infested guy! I'm very clean!"

"Don't worry, Andrew. She's just being a little immature."

"You're the one who thought I should like her."

"I think I may have been wrong about that."

Then Genny asked me about something I really didn't want to talk about. "Andrew," she started. "Why didn't you tell me that you've been hanging out with MacKenzie a lot? I think that's great news. So why would you keep it from me?"

"What? I haven't been hanging out with MacKenzie."

"Yes, you have. Gus told me all about it."

"Oh. He did?"

"Yes, I know that you eat lunch with her every day. So what is going on?"

"Um. Nothing."

"You know, if that is the case, you have to ask her to that dance before she really does get a date."

"Oh, it's too late. She already has a date."

"Andrew!!! Gus told me she doesn't. What is going on with you? You are acting super-strange. Did Rebecca from Texas somehow put a not-yourself spell on you?"

"No! She didn't!" I was really getting nervous. I went to rub my hair, but knocked off my glasses. I tripped over my own feet when I attempted to get up off the bed. I started to stutter! "I d-d-d-d-don't want to, to, to talk about this!"

"I can help you, though, Andrew. I'm here to do just that. I can coach you through asking her to the dance. I thought that's what you wanted me to do!"

"It's not what I want you, what I want y-y-y-you to do anymore. Can't you see that?" I was losing it. Really losing it. I hoped she wouldn't push me any further. Oh, but she did.

She was getting a little upset, too. Loud and exasperated, she said, "Well, then, what *do* you want? Will you please tell me what's going on, because I'm wringing my ponytail trying to fig-ure it out on my own. I can't help you anymore, Andrew. What do you want me to do?"

"Nothing. Please, just stay right here."

"Well, I already do that. What is going on?"

"Genny, can't you see that I don't even care about MacKenzie anymore? Can't you tell that I never talk about her like I used to? The only crush I have is totally and completely on *you*!"

I ran out the door and around the block. I ran and ran and ran. I couldn't believe what I had just told Genny. I couldn't believe everything that was happening. I had fallen hard . . . for a genie.

Chapter 16
"I Am Allergic to Love!"
by Genny the Genie

Oh my goodness, oh my goodness.

If Rebecca had stopped screaming for just one second during this assignment, maybe I would have gotten the hint. Maybe I wouldn't have been blinder than a dead bat about Andrew. He likes me!???

Oh my goodness, oh my goodness. This is not a good thing. In fact, he has no idea how bad this could be. I could lose my genie license! He could get his heart broken!

"GENNY AND ANDREW, SITTIN' IN A TREE. K-I-S-S-I-N-G!" Rebecca was really tormenting me. Unfortunately, she had heard the whole entire, totally embarrassing love scene. "FIRST COMES LOVE, SECOND COMES MARRIAGE, THEN GENNY WILL BE HOLDING HER FIRED GENIE PAPERS!"

I rushed to put on Andrew's earmuffs. I turned on his CD player. Even though I hated techno, I played it loud to muffle her taunting. I just couldn't take her right now. Catfish pranced around the room, his hair standing on end. He knew this situation could easily spell disaster. Even Throttle was quaking up and down — he thought we should leave immediately. Genies are *not* allowed to date their masters. *Never, ever, ever.* But I would never leave my master — especially when he needed me the most. Or wait — maybe Andrew needed to see a little less of me. Oh my goodness!

In all of my years, no kid master of mine had ever fallen in love with me. Okay, I think Abe Lincoln kinda-sorta liked me — but at least he never told me so! This was sooo not good. Me!!!? Andrew likes *moi*!? I proceeded to freak for about five more minutes. Then I had to adjust my ponytail and start thinking straight. This was a big mess, and I, being the genie and all, would have to fix it. Even though I'm not supposed to feel this way, I did kind of like Andrew maybe more than I should have. I cannot lie about that. I definitely felt a warm, close bond with him that I hardly ever have with real people. But a crush? Honestly, the thought hadn't even crossed my mind — maybe because I would never let it. I wouldn't consider liking one of my masters in a million years. Not ever, ever, ever! That's totally against the rules.

It just goes to show that I should never be paired with boys. I just don't get them at all. If I understood guys better, maybe I would have seen this coming. But I totally don't, so what am I going to do?

Oh my goodness.

I had so many feelings all at once. In another time — like more than one thousand years ago when I was a real girl — it might have worked for Andrew and me. But under these circumstances, romance was nothing but doomed. I know other genies who are older than thirteen — they're like in their twenties at least! — who have left the geniehood for love. I have even been tempted once or twice (not with my masters, mind you). But when you're my age, you can't leave your whole life for love. At least not these days. Sure, people got married when they were fourteen back in my day — but no one does that anymore. When you're my age — that is, thirteen — getting super-seriously involved romantically isn't a smart idea. What do you really know about love when you're thirteen? I know I've been thirteen for more than one thousand years, and I still have wagonloads to learn.

So does Andrew. I don't want to be the one to teach him about heartache. I don't want him to remember me that way! But I can't let this go on for even another second. This crush on me has to stop. So how do I end it without hurting him? He is so near and dear to my heart. Maybe that is the problem — we became too bosom of buddies. Why did I let this happen? Why, oh why, oh why?

I told myself to think fast because as quick as Andrew runs, he could be back home in a flash. I thought and thought and thought. My mind was totally blank. I reached for one of Catfish's Q-Tips, twirled it in my fingers, and *voilà*! Something came to me. Ahhh, yes . . .

I knew what I had to do, even if it would break *my* heart, which this plan I just thought up would definitely do. It was actually very easy; all I had to do was heed my own advice.

There was a week and a half left before that dance. I knew I had better stop sitting in Andrew's room watching TV and having heart-to-hearts with my master. Boy, all that did was get me into trouble. I was going to be busy. I had to: a) Make sure Andrew was totally over me; b) Get him back with MacKenzie; and c) Patch up things with Jane!

"HA-HA-HA-HA-HA-HA! Andrew is in *wuv*! Andrew wants to smooch *you*!" Rebecca still taunted.

"Shut up!!!" I yelled at her as I dropped some baby powder into Throttle. Hee-hee. That made her sneeze.

In silence, I prepared myself for Andrew's return.

Chapter 17

"Love Is Really a Roller Coaster"

by Andrew

Maybe she will like me, I thought as I made my way back to my house. I had run three whole miles and I wasn't even tired yet. My nerves pumped through my body, on a mission to keep me from relaxing. The thump-thump sound of my heart was enough to make me go loony. But anxious or not, I realized I had to go back to my room — where Genny was surely waiting for me. I bit my tongue and sluggishly headed home. Part of me was scared and embarrassed to face her again. The other part of me was dying to find out what Genny would say — hopefully she'd say she felt the same way I did.

My head was still spinning. I really should have checked my horoscope before I went around professing my crush. I hoped the planets were all in favor of me having a good crush day. I began to wonder which was worse: her liking me or her not liking me. If she did, then I didn't know what to do. I'd never known anyone who has had a genie for a girlfriend. Like, where do you take a genie on a date? Mine had already been around the world fifty times — surely a visit to the zoo would be kinda dull. And taking her to the Sarasota museum? Not only had she already seen all of van Gogh's paintings, she watched him paint them. Making a girl happy was hard enough — just wait until you start hanging out with a genie!

And if she *didn't* like me? What would I do then? I knew exactly what would happen: I would shrivel up and die inside. But I had to be optimistic. Genny had told me all of these things, like how cute I was, and how all the girls would be silly not to fall for me. I hoped that meant she had a crush on *moi*, too. Why else would she say all of those things? I thought I'd liked MacKenzie a lot, but that was nothing compared to how I felt about Genny! I didn't try to feel this way; I definitely didn't mean to. It's just that the more we hung out, the deeper I fell.

Finally, even after walking as humanly, painstakingly slow as possible, I was at the doorway to my bedroom. I felt doomed. I didn't know what was about to happen. My hands shook as I reached for the knob. I reminded myself that I had to do it. A guy can't be afraid of going into his own room for the rest of his life.

I opened the door. And it was . . . A BIG MESS!

"Hey, boy, what's up with you?" Genny said, hugging me. I had to back away because she smelled like really dirty kitty litter. She was trying to eat potato chips, but she kept missing her mouth. So crumbs and spit were all over her chin, and the chips were all over my bed. Also, for some strange reason, all of the clothes in my closet were strewn all over the floor.

"What happened in here? What happened to *you*?" I asked in disbelief.

"Oh, your closet just threw up," she said. "All over me."

"Huh? What are you talking about?" She usually made perfect sense, but she was talking like she needed to be locked up.

I looked at my walls, and much to my horror, my Atlanta Braves flags had been torn down.

"Hey, where are my Braves flags?"

"Oh, I hate the things; I threw them in the trash."

"What? You did *WHAT*?!!!" This was all just too weird for me. You tell a girl you like her, and she completely loses her mind. It just didn't seem appropriate for me to bring up the subject. "Did you have to tear up my Braves stuff?"

"I told you I hated it. Oh, Andrew, I picked out a movie you and I should watch together. It's called *How to Eat Dirty Kitty Litter Without Throwing Up*."

"Ewww, gross," I said. What was it with her and the kitty litter today? She smelled so bad I couldn't watch a movie with her even if I had wanted to. Really, since my room had turned into *The Twilight Zone*, all I wanted to do was leave ASAP.

Was this the same genie I just professed my love to?

"You don't wanna snuggle up and watch a movie with me?" she asked pathetically as she inhaled a huge handful of potato chips and snorted a few of them out through her nose.

"Genny, I don't know what's going on here, but I have to go."

I was heading straight to I-don't-know-where. I wished I could go to Gus's, but things just weren't the same between us. I just had to get out of there, like, yesterday. My heart ached because it had been put through such an up-and-down workout today. My emotions were completely drained. I really did love the old

Genny. But I didn't know about this girl covered in cat poo.

"Why are you leaving?"

"What is wrong with you?" I asked. But before she could answer, I escaped from the psychoticness that was going on in my bedroom. I slammed the door and ran down the street.

Chapter 18
"Genny – That's Me – Goes to Class"
by Genny the Genie

I knew Throttle couldn't breathe, so I untangled him from the layers upon layers of shorts and jackets that I had wrapped him in. There had to be a better way to silence Rebecca. I couldn't keep suffocating Throttle just to muffle her screams. If only I could find more magic sleeping dust. She just had to be quiet, because I knew that the second she got the chance, she'd tell Andrew exactly what I was up to. He couldn't find out my plan — which was to be as disgusting as humanly possible in order to make him fall out of love with me. Who wants to spend time with someone who smells worse than an unhygienic, homeless feline? I knew I'd have to add more grossness to my charade so he'll make the right —

far less heartbreaking — decision to crush on MacKenzie instead of me.

As sure as the Romans live in Rome, Rebecca began her screaming. I threw on the earmuffs and put Catfish's kitty muffs on him. Ahhh, much better. I couldn't stand my stinking, unappetizing self, so I took a shower. I did some aerobics — I love my old friend Jane Fonda and her first workout tapes — so I would wear myself completely out. I wanted to sleep for a thousand years so I didn't have to think about Andrew. Plus, I wanted to be out cold when he came back home. I went to bed — and I didn't get out of Throttle until Andrew had left the next morning for school.

I heard him go down the stairs and shut the door behind him. He hopped on his bike and headed to Sarasota Middle School. That's where I was going in a few minutes, too. I hopped in the shower (no one was home), put on my shiniest lip gloss, and fixed my hair. I spent way too much time primping, but I like to look nice even if no one is going to see me. (I'm invisible to everyone except Andrew, Gus, and Jane.)

I was going to the school on a genie-spy mission. I needed to see this MacKenzie girl for myself. If I was going to — finally — get down to business and fix her up with my sweet Andrew, she had better be a good, nice girl. I would have to have a better plan if she wasn't every bit as cool and sweet as Andrew said she was.

I showed up right when they were eating lunch. I hid behind the trash cans — so Andrew wouldn't spot me — to watch MacKenzie and him eat together. Wow, that girl was striking, but maybe not the way you would think. See, she wasn't the most beautiful girl I'd ever seen, not the way Jane was, but MacKenzie was still unique. She didn't have perfect almond-shaped eyes or the best nose in the world. She didn't have flawless skin or hair. That's not what matters anyway — I was never a beauty queen, either. It was something else about MacKenzie that made her beautiful. Maybe it was that winning, warm smile. Or those eyes, which had more sparkle and curiosity in them than a diamond waiting to be expertly cut. She and Andrew laughed a lot and had a good time. She leaned toward him to listen intently every time he said a word.

Gus and Jane weren't sitting too far away. They looked like they were in their own world. Gus really cared about his friend, you could tell by the way he watched her and listened to her. Not that anyone could take their eyes away from her face, the girl was gorgeous. I started to see why her hair was cut so badly — I think she wanted it that way. Yes, I have met her type before. Jane is the supersharp kind of chick who wants to be noticed for her brain, not her beauty. You have to admire a girl for that, although she should learn to love her looks. Hmmm. . . . I started to hope I'd get my hands on her.

I spent the day poking around the middle school and watching the kids. I never went to school, so the whole system is fascinating to me. I would have loved to go to a place like school where I could learn about literature, science, and social studies. We didn't know much about any of that stuff back when I was mortal. But at least my *papa*, who was a wizard, taught me everything he could at home (like astrology and magic and vegetable-ology). See, when I was a preteen, girls were strictly forbidden to get an education. According to the law, we were put on earth to cook good rabbit's head stews, have at least ten babies, and then make scratchy clothes out of old potato sacks. Yes, it stunk. So my daddy home-schooled me — he didn't want a peasant's life for me. That's actually how I became a genie in the first place, to make a really, really long story short.

I could spend weeks at America's public

schools. Unfortunately, I only had that day. I went to an eighth-grade chemistry class and learned about the properties of mercury. Then I headed to home ec, where kids were putting the finishing touches on their pot holders. I spent some time in a math class and watched the teacher solve some really hard problems. And last, I headed to band class — where the girls who played the piccolo reminded me of my most recent master, Sophie. When the final bell of the day rang, I went by the tennis courts, where some kids had set up a skateboard track.

That's where I found MacKenzie. She was doing loop-de-loops and all kinds of fancy, scary stuff. I listened to her talk to her friends. "I can't stay long," she said.

One friend replied, "I thought you didn't candy-stripe today."

"I don't, but I need to read some mail to this little old lady who is dying and lonely at the hospital."

MacKenzie's friends told her she was amazing.

Okay, so she *was* good enough for Andrew. I walked over to her backpack and slipped Andrew's business card — the ones he made up for his homework business — into the front pocket. I had written on the back of it, "M, Call me sometime. ☺ Andrew."

Although things couldn't have been going better — MacKenzie seemed to like Andrew, plus she was a nice girl — completing this part of my plan made me sad. I couldn't help it — my true feelings just are what they are. I was jealous of this MacKenzie girl . . . she was the lucky girl who would get to hang out with Andrew.

Chapter 19
"You Never Woulda Thunk It"
by Andrew

Genny still hadn't talked to me about what I said to her. I tell her I have a crush on her, and she stops taking baths and starts spraying half-chewed food out of her mouth. Is this the effect I have on girls? I hoped when I got home from school, she would be normal. I needed her to be the Genny I fell for in the first place.

I didn't have such good luck. When I walked in my bedroom she was scratching her armpits. She was wearing my old, ripped-up sweatpants that were ten sizes too big for her. Her hair had brown, gooey gunkballs in it. What was up with her?

"Andrew, maybe we need to talk a little bit."

"I totally agree," I said. I got close to her, and she smelled like garlic. I mean, she *really* smelled like four-day-old, moldy, tangy garlic. "Do you want to get cleaned up first?"

"Cleaned up? I am cleaned up!"

"You have goo in your hair, Genny."

"No I don't! I just washed it. Are you saying I'm dirty? Are you? Are you?"

"Um, no, I would never say that about you."

"Well, you better not!" she proclaimed as she picked something off the bottom of her shoe and ate it. My stomach almost turned right then and there. "Anyway, I want to talk."

"Me too," I said, although I wasn't sure I really wanted to have this conversation with her right that second. She wasn't the Genny I had a huge crush on.

"Okay, let's figure this out. You like me," she said as she reached up her shirt, scratched her armpit, then smelled her finger, "and you like MacKenzie. Well, you can't like us both. So I need you to make a decision." She had green bits of food stuck in all of her teeth.

At that moment, I was numb. It hurt me inside out to lose the Genny I loved. But this girl — er, thing — sitting in my bedroom with me wasn't Genny. If I could have the old one, the decision would be easy to make.

"Genny, I liked you the way you were."

"Well, dolly, this is me now. This is the way

I've always been. I was putting on a show for you before — but if you're going to like me, you need to know how I really am. This is it! Now, you take me as is, or you can go straight to heck!"

I couldn't say a word. I didn't like her one bit. She stunk like moldy garlic, plus she was being a witch. I started to long for MacKenzie, who was a normal, cool girl. One who I really, really liked. But I didn't know what to say. "I, um," I said, "Genny, I need some time to think."

With that, she stomped off into her bottle, saying nasty putdowns about boys being the scum of the earth.

Then the phone rang. Miraculously — I think the heavens had it planned — MacKenzie called me at just that moment.

"Andrew?"

"Hey!" I said, genuinely excited to talk to a normal girl.

"What's up?"

She told me the sad story about the dying lady at the hospital. She told me about her skateboarding expo. Then she wanted to know if I was busy next weekend.

"No, I'm not busy. That's just the dance, and I'm not going to it."

"Oh, well, me neither."

"You're not?" I asked, relieved to hear that she still didn't have a date.

"No. I don't have anyone to go with."

"Me neither."

"Andrew? Um, do you want to maybe go together?"

Day of all days! This one was weird!!! I have been hot on the trail of MacKenzie Brown for at least a million years. I have admired her from afar, and she had completely ignored me. Only in the last two weeks — when I fell supernaturally for a genie — has MacKenzie given me the time of day. Then, of all the freaky things in the world, the girl — MACKENZIE — was asking *me* to the eighth-grade dance.

I literally fell off my bed.

"Are you okay?" she asked after hearing the commotion.

"Um, no . . . I'm afraid I just broke my toe. Can I call you right back?"

"Yeah, sure," she said.

"Okay, bye," I replied.

"Wait, you don't have my number." She proceeded to give it to me, although I had looked up her digits in the phone book four years ago — and have had her number memorized ever since. "Bye."

I gathered myself together — the hurt toe

was a little white lie so I could have a minute or two to think. I couldn't stand it another second. I called up my old friend Gus.

"What's up, Andrew?" he said. I could hear Jane there in the background. It made me sad because usually after school, the three of us would hang out at Gus's together. But I wasn't invited anymore.

"I have to talk to you. I have to. Please, please, I need some major advice."

"Okay, okay, man. But Jane and I are in the middle of setting everything up for tomorrow's first FFD meeting. Can you call me back later?"

"No! I can't! I'm begging you, Gus. Just talk to me for a second. It's best if Jane can't hear you."

"Okay, wait a second." I heard Gus switch telephones.

"Listen," I frantically said.

"Slow down and breathe, Andrew."

"I can't! MacKenzie — MACKENZIE — just asked me to the eighth-grade dance."

"No way. You're kidding. You are just smooth lately, Drew. What have you been doing? Listening to old soul tunes? Using even mintier mouthwash?"

"I'm not joking, Gus. She asked me!"

"So what's the problem? That's great news, right? What did you tell her?"

"I told her I broke my toe, and that I'd call her back."

"Have you been sniffing too much garbage? Are you out of your mind? Why didn't you say you'd go?"

"Well, I have another problem."

"What could be the problem? Your dream woman just asked you to the biggest dance of our lives."

"Here's the problem. . . . Um, I've, um, been crushing on Genny."

Gus was silent.

"Well, say something!" I demanded.

He started laughing. "I'm sorry," he said. "It's not funny."

"No, it's not!"

"But I just have visions of you boogying down with an invisible girl at the dance. You'll be in the corner talking to yourself. And at the end of the evening, people will see you giving your invisible date a kiss." He kept giggling.

"That's not funny! You and I can see her. That's all that matters!"

"How are you going to introduce her to your parents, man? Even if they do believe you, do you think they're going to let you keep living with her in your bedroom? What a mess that will be!"

97

He was right; those things hadn't crossed my mind.

"Another thing, Andrew . . . Genny's only going to be here for a short time. So even if you *are* in love with her, you're never going to see her again. MacKenzie, on the other hand, will be around forever. You'll even see her in high school. You need to think about this whole thing practically."

"You're absolutely right. I owe you."

"Yeah, yeah, yeah. You're welcome. I have the opposite problem. Too many girls have asked me to go to the dance, and I had to tell them I couldn't." He said he didn't have crushes on the girls who had crushes on him. I asked him if he was still going to the dance, and thankfully, he said he was. But it was weird — Gus sounded sad when he said he and Jane were going together — he said they'd miss having me around. He and I talked for a few more minutes, then I told him I had to go.

"Mmmm, mmmm, MacKenzie," I stammered after I'd dialed the phone and she'd picked up.

"Hi, Andrew!"

"I would, I would, I would loooove to go to the dance with you."

Chapter 20
"I Know This Will Work"
by Genny the Genie

I am so filthy that I'm grossing myself out. It is ridiculous to roll around in kitty litter and eat poo off your shoe. Okay, so I put some chocolate on my shoe . . . Andrew didn't know that. And I can tell my whole plan is working like a charm.

I just keep acting as yucky as I can whenever he's around. It breaks my heart that my tricks are working. Andrew isn't in love with me anymore. He just thinks I'm cuckoo. The good thing is, he's going to the dance with MacKenzie this weekend. He's been back to his old self lately, too. He picks through trash at the mansions; he does homework papers for other people all night long; and he's been going to track practice. I miss our hanging-out time. But this way is so much better. He won't be hurt when I'm gone . . . if I still smell like this, I'm sure he'll be relieved.

He did a really sweet thing this evening. He surprised Gus and went to the FFD meeting.

"Why you goin'?" I asked him.

"Gus means the world to me, so if this is what I have to do for us to be real friends again, I'll do it. Can I borrow some needles and thread?"

I gave him a whole sewing kit, and packed it with gorgeous materials for him to give to Gus. "Tell him those are from me." I loved Gus. Andrew winced from my stench when he got close to me.

"What are you going to do about Jane?" I asked.

"I'm going to smother her with kindness until she forgives me," he said as he went out the door. He was too sweet and too cute. I hoped he'd have some luck.

I had a plan to help him along, though. I washed the mashed, stinky broccoli off my body, and put on some pretty, clean clothes. I hate being so disgusting!

So I went on the genie-net and ordered another box of chocolates. I made another 1700s-style valentine. In calligraphy, I wrote the words that were on page three million, four hundred and seventy-three. The words were, "You are special. These are for you." I signed it, "From Andrew." That little move, if carried out perfectly, was one-hundred-percent guaranteed to cast a love spell over their date. They would have a wonderful time at the dance, I just knew it.

I hugged Catfish and cried a wee, tiny bit. (Don't tell anyone!)

Chapter 21
"I'm a Dance Dork! Help!"
by Andrew

Genny had disappeared. I heard her yelling at Rebecca a lot. Maybe that evil Texas ex-genie was keeping her busy. Whatever she was up to, I hoped that Genny was winning.

I couldn't help it, I missed Genny — even though she had become one-hundred-percent pigpen. Dirty or not, I still wanted us to be friends. I never should have told her how I felt; that's when everything changed. She never smelled like dead fish before then. And her behavior was fishy, too. I wished I could take back the whole incident. We'd all be better off if I had just kept my big, lovey-dovey mouth shut.

I needed Genny! If I held my nose, I thought maybe she could give me some good advice before this dance. I couldn't help but be totally nervous. Tonight, I was going out with one of the most beautiful women in all of the surrounding counties.

I couldn't believe my own genie wasn't here on the biggest evening of my life. I stood in my room and said, "Genny, where are you? I am your master, and I need you to come out!" I hadn't commanded her to do anything, so I felt kind of bad about being bossy. But I knew her time was up soon. I couldn't just leave things the way they were — then never see her again!

She didn't show up. And I was disappointed. I went through my clothes — I needed something cool to wear. I would have asked Gus for some fashion advice, but I had thought Genny would be here to help me. She *used* to be my personal fashion queen. I figured Gus would have to take over again soon. At least things between he and I were really good now. I was still working on Jane, though. I'd made some progress — she was looking at me now, and she stopped screaming in public that I had mice in my bedroom. She was coming around. It was just a bit weird that she was going to the dance with Gus. I felt like they'd been up to fun things, and I hadn't been invited to the festivities. I missed the three of us.

I found a little surprise in my closet. There

was a nice brand-new suit. It looked like it came straight out of *GQ* magazine. The shirt underneath was a spiffy blue button-down. The tie was shiny and striped; it looked like something Brad Pitt would wear. I had never seen a suit like that, let alone put one on. The boutonniere was already pinned into the pocket. It was a yellow daisy. A bouquet of matching flowers appeared on my bed. I swear it wasn't there when I first looked.

A white rectangular box was sitting right next to the cute wrist bouquet. It had an elaborate card attached. I read it. Weird. There were instructions. *Give this to MacKenzie, and repeat the words on the card.*

Genny poofed before my eyes. She said, "Don't worry about a thing. The night will be magical and awesome."

She looked so beautiful, and she didn't smell.

"I can't stay long, but I wanted to make sure you got everything."

"I did — thanks for the suit and the flowers."

"Oh, no problem."

"But what's with the boxes of candy?"

"Just please, please, please, follow those instructions to a T."

"Um, okay."

"Okay, I've got to run. Oh, one more important thing . . . here . . ." She disappeared for a few more seconds. She handed me a book about marine biology — Jane's favorite subject. "I found this in my box of books. Give this to Jane and tell her you're sorry."

"I've told her that a million times."

"Tell her again. Things will be different to-night. Then I need you to say one more thing. The magic words are: 'Let's all just be best friends forever. This time I mean it.'"

"I can't say that to her."

"Say it! I swear! She will definitely thank you for it. Trust me."

"Okay."

"Do you promise to do everything?"

"I promise."

She poofed away, taking her screaming bottle with her. I watched her hair flow in the wind until she disappeared.

Chapter 22
"I Love Pretending That I'm Jane's Genie!"
by Genny the Genie

Andrew was too, too cute. It was probably good that I didn't get to see him in his suit. I whipped it up over the last few days, which is why he hadn't seen me very much. Also, I was having a particularly hard time keeping Rebecca quiet. I had to keep her away from Andrew so she wouldn't ruin my plan. Finally, I had the idea to make an ex-genie muzzle. It sounds a little barbaric, but really, it's a very humane way to keep people's mouths shut. I learned it in the eleventh century. I made a silk band that fits perfectly around her head. It's tight enough so she can't move her jaws much — but she *can* sip through a straw. She still screeches — and makes noises that don't have any meaning. But she cannot taunt me — or tell Andrew what I'm up to. When the bow's on her head, I put a sleeveless sweater on her. She cannot move her hands up enough to mess with the band on her head. When people are around, I put the ex-genie muzzle on her. When we're alone, I take it off — and don't make her wear it. After all, I don't want to be accused of ex-genie abuse! The Genie Council would understand if they knew what this Texan has put me through. For now, the whole solution is working pretty nicely — at least, it'll do until I find some more magic sleeping dust or some other way to solve this problem.

She was nice and quiet when I took her to Jane's. I had to bring her and Throttle because all of my beauty supplies were in there. I couldn't wait to bring out that girl's natural beauty. Her inner beauty was already evident — except when she was putting down Andrew. (But hey, hurt can cause us all to do crazy things.)

I arrived and she was already wearing a dress. It was paisley, and so not flattering. It was shiny material, but it hung from her shoulders to her hips like a paper bag. I'm glad I planned ahead.

"I do like your dress, but would you like to look at a few I brought for you?" I had made a bunch for her to choose from.

"Yeah, I guess."

"Also, girl, let me do your hair. Do you mind if I give you a bit of a trim? I think you need some shape to that shiny hair."

"Um, okay, I just don't want to be late."

She talked about amazing sea turtles she'd seen at four A.M. on the beach. She described the colorful striped fish she had caught on the pier. I heard about the FFD and the other things in school she loves. She and Gus had been doing *everything* together.

I said, "I wish I was human, so I could be best friends with Gus . . . and Andrew, too."

"Yes, I'm a very lucky girl," she said. "I've got some amazing friends," she said as I quickly snip, snip, snipped her hair. Then I changed the subject. We talked about music and sports and our favorite stars. Of course, then the subject of Andrew came up. She admitted to me that she can't really hate him. I begged her to give him another chance. I said that he really wanted to be friends with her. Then I told her the honest-to-goodness truth: "You are so cute!"

I finished her hair — I put it in a short, boyish pixie cut. That was much better than the chin-length mop she had, *excusez* my French. Her face was so strikingly perfect, she really didn't need any hair at all. I told her that. "You could be bald and people wouldn't be able to take their eyes off you."

"Oh, stop," she said and genuinely blushed.

She chose to wear a bright red dress. I thought it suited her vibrant personality. It was formfitting, with spaghetti straps, and arm-length red gloves to match. I handed her a ruby ring and told her to wear it. "This belonged to the real Princess Grace Kelly. I want you to wear it. It will make you feel more confident about your looks. I only lend it to my favorite beauty princesses."

Her eyes went so wide I thought those big blue suckers were going to fall out of their sockets. She hugged me and thanked me. Finally, this girl, who usually looked as frumpy as possible, looked like a model. I wanted her to experience one night of showing her outer beauty, since she was so pretty on the inside already. (Which was most of the time — especially when she wasn't torturing Andrew.) Making people feel good about themselves is one of my favorite parts of the job.

Before I left, I had just one more thing to do. I held her hand and said, "I have to cast this spell on you."

"Spell? Do I need a spell?"

"No, you will have a wonderful time without my help. But if you let me do this just once, I'll be able to sleep tonight. See, I have a superstitious side."

"Well, okay."

I proceeded, "Neehow, bleehow, seehow." I wiggled my hips and tapped my left big toe four times. "I'm done!"

"That was fast. What was that for?"

"Oh, just to help you have the time of your life." I just didn't think it would hurt to cast a little harmless memory-making spell. So that's exactly what I did.

I hugged her and poofed away.

Chapter 23
"I Survived the Eighth-Grade Dance"
by Andrew

"Look at your fancy duds," Gus said, eyeing me ear to toe. I have to admit it, I looked so good. I was even more stylin' than him.

"You don't look so bad yourself." Gus knew he looked great — he always looked that way. For once, though, I think I had one-upped him in the clothing department.

"Did Genny dress you today?"

"She even *made* this suit for me."

"Still in love with the genie?"

I felt a love pang when he said it. But I surely wasn't going to listen to him laugh because I liked a genie again. "I'm over her; I'm into MacKenzie."

"Cool, man. That girl is into you. I've seen the way she waits to eat lunch with you every day.

Listen, I'm sorry that I haven't liked her. I know she's really pretty cool. Just don't go out with her and forget about us — me and Jane, you know."

"I won't, I promise. It's weird that she finally seems to like me, though, huh? Who woulda thunk it?"

"Yeah, a lot of things are weird."

"I agree with you completely."

I knew exactly how he felt. We bonded while we got ready at his house. We also did some much-needed catching up. After watching Gus do his hair for like half an hour, we were driven by his mom to Jane's, then MacKenzie's, and off to the eighth-grade dance we went.

MacKenzie looked amazing. So did Jane. I don't know what my good friend did to her hot self, but even Gus almost dropped dead because she was so gorgeous. It was really odd to see Jane in a flattering red dress. Maybe she should dress up more often. Gus seemed glad she was around; he needed Jane super-bad that night. She helped him fend off the women. I had no clue how popular Gus had become with the ladies. Some guys have it early — but Gus didn't like any of them as more than friends. Oh well!

I made up with Jane right away. And I told her that she was my best friend, and that's what

I wanted us to always be. I gave her the book Genny gave me. She loved it — I know because she hugged me.

"Andrew, don't worry about it anymore. I'm over you," she said. "Gus was right, you and I are too much like family. That's how I want us to be, too."

Whew! I was glad to get that settled. I went over to MacKenzie and gave her the box of candy. I said everything Genny told me to say. I'm not usually superstitious, but I think it worked! The night was more perfect than a dance scene in a teen movie!

MacKenzie was really digging me. I didn't feel the way I used to about her. I mean, don't get me wrong, I still had a huge crush. But I had made her out to be an absolutely flawless goddess. She wasn't — she was just a teenage girl. But more than that, MacKenzie was real and kind and cute. So I definitely still liked her, but in a more genuine way. All of a sudden, something dawned on me: I think I was growing up.

MacKenzie and I slow-danced and fast-danced. We laughed every second. When her favorite song came on, *it* happened. We kissed. It was my first one, and I was nervous.

She told me that she wished she hadn't wasted all of those years.

"What are you talking about?" I asked as I began to worry if I had fresh, minty breath.

"I have been missing out. I should have liked you all along."

I smiled at her. MacKenzie really was a cool, sweet chick. I was so happy that she finally came to her senses. She wasn't lying — I could tell she liked me!

Wow.

Chapter 24
"Why Do Things Have to End?"
by Genny the Genie

I have a few more days left, but I think my job is done. Every wish has been granted, and Catfish just reported to me that the dance couldn't have been more perfect. So I cannot stay; I have already helped Andrew accomplish his goals. He is very happy — with his friends and his crush. I packed my stuff and tried to get out of there as quickly as I could. I was afraid I'd never leave if I saw Andrew, Gus, and Jane again. I liked them so much; I would have given almost anything to be human and be able to be their real friends.

It was hard to go! But that's what my life is like — it can be very hard to be a genie. I reached into Throttle and left Andrew's Atlanta Braves flags on his bed. I wouldn't really rip them up. I wanted him to have them back.

Just as I was poofing away, I found some-thing on Andrew's dresser for me. There was a letter wrapped around a cassette tape. I took it back into Throttle. I put on the tape — it was the Beatles — and read the note before I fell asleep. I will let the letter speak for itself. Andrew just has such a way with words!

Dear Genny the Genie,

I want you to know how much I appreciate the suit, the flowers, and all of the other stuff. We went through a lot, and I'm glad I had the chance to get to know you. Not because you're a genie with amazing stories and a few special powers, but because you're a fabulous, unique, and wonderful person. Genny, you know, you will always be a human first, and a genie second.

I recently realized you rolled around in kitty litter just to throw me off. I know you said catty things just so I wouldn't like you anymore. I will always wonder what would have happened with us if you weren't a genie.

Please remember me forever! I will never for-get you.

Love,
Andrew

Smiling, I fell into a deep sleep.

About the Author

Kristen Kemp is the author of several books about Genny the Genie, as well as other Scholastic titles, such as the 2 Grrrls guides. She stays busy writing for women's and teen magazines and is currently a contributing editor at *YM*. She lives in Saratoga Springs, NY, with her husband, Steve, their dog, Clipper, and two cats. In her spare time, she loves to visit her hometown in Indiana.